Enid Blyton

LIBRARIES NI
WITHDRAWN FROM STOCK

The Seaside Family

The Family Series

D1438432

EGMONT

CHAPTER ONE
Summer Holidays Again

'School's over for two months, thank goodness!' said Mike, and he slammed his books down on the table. The vase of flowers there nearly jumped off the table. 'Mike! Be careful,' said Mummy. 'There now – Belinda has done the same – and off goes the vase.'

'Sorry Mummy,' said Belinda, and picked up the vase. Mike went to get a cloth to wipe up the water. Ann picked up the flowers. They were all laughing. Mummy couldn't help laughing too.

'Well I know how you feel, when school is ended for a time,' she said. 'The summer holidays are so lovely and long for you too, aren't they – almost eight weeks. Goodness me

– what shall I do with you for eight weeks?'

'I know what I want to do,' said Mike. 'I want to go to the seaside. We've been in a houseboat on a canal . . .'

'And we've been on a big ship for a trip,' said Ann.

'And now we want to go to the seaside,' said Mike. 'Don't we, girls?'

'Yes,' said the girls at once, and Mummy smiled. 'You've been planning this together on the way home from school!' she said. 'Well, it's no good asking *me*. It's Daddy you must ask. It costs money to go to the seaside, you know, and we don't have very much to spare.'

'Mummy, we don't see why it should cost very much to go and stay at the seaside,' said Mike, earnestly. 'Can't we go in our caravans? Then we don't need to take a house anywhere, or to go to a hotel. We'd just live in the caravans as usual.'

Mike's family had two caravans that stood in a green field where cows grazed. Sometimes the cows bumped against the vans at night and woke the children – but they didn't mind little things like that! That was all part of the fun.

The caravans were painted red and yellow. They had little red chimneys out of which smoke came when Mummy lighted her fire, or got the stove going in the children's caravan.

Mike, Belinda and Ann slept in three bunks, one above the other in one caravan. Mummy and Daddy slept in bunks in the other caravan. It was fun.

The children lived at school from Monday to Friday in the term-time, and came back to the caravans for the weekends. How they loved that! What fun it was to have a home on wheels, one that had no roots, but could be taken anywhere they liked.

'We'll ask Daddy as soon as we see him,' said Mike. 'We'll *make* him say yes. He'll love it too.'

So they lay in wait for Daddy, and hurled themselves on him as soon as he walked in at the field-gate.

'Daddy! We've something to ask you.'

'Something very important!'

'Something you've *got* to say yes to!'

'Is it something about the summer holidays?' asked Daddy thinking that three children could be very very heavy when they all hung on to him at once.

'Yes,' said everyone.

'Well, before you begin, let me break the news to you,' said Daddy firmly. 'Whatever ideas you've got in your head have got to come out. I've no money to spend on a summer holiday by the sea! That is – if you want to go to a hotel. The only thing I can do for you this summer is to let you go away somewhere fresh and new in the caravans. Nothing else at all.'

The three children squealed loudly.

'But *Daddy!* That's what we WANT! We want to go to the sea in the caravans. It's what we wanted to ask you.'

'Well, well, well – great minds certainly do think alike!' said Daddy. 'I must ask Mummy about it first.'

'We've asked her, we've asked her!' chanted Ann. 'And she said we must ask you. And we've asked *you*. So is it settled?'

Daddy began to laugh. 'What a lot of little pests you are! Yes, yes – it's settled. We'll choose a nice seaside place, and we'll all go off there together. I shall enjoy it too. But wait a minute – I've just thought of something.'

'What?' said all three alarmed.

'It's this – I've asked Ben Johns to come and stay with you here,' said Daddy. 'I meant to put him up in the farmer's cottage and let him

6

play with you all day. Oh dear – what shall we do about that?'

By this time Mummy was with them. 'Oh – little Ben Johns?' she said. 'Yes, I remember we said we'd have him for a time. Poor child, his mother's very ill, isn't she? Well – we can't very well go to the seaside then.'

'We can! We can take him too!' said Belinda. 'Just another bunk put up in our caravan, that's all! We've three already. Can't you get another one just for these holidays, Daddy?'

'Yes – I suppose we could,' said Daddy, and everyone cheered. 'Now – I want my TEA! Who's going to get it? And afterwards we'll settle everything.'

'More fun!' cried Belinda, running to make the tea. 'More fun for the Caravan Family!'

CHAPTER TWO
Benjy Comes Along

It was great fun planning the seaside holiday.
They got out maps and pored over them.

'Let's go to the east coast,' said Mummy. 'It's
so healthy.'

'Too cold for me,' said Daddy, 'Let's go to
the west coast.'

'What's this little place down here?' said
Belinda, pointing to where a bit of land
curved out and made a small bay. 'It looks
lovely here – on the south coast.'

'That's Sea-gull Cove,' said Mike, reading
the name printed in very small letters. 'What
a lovely name!'

'Sea-gull Cove!' said Daddy, suddenly

looking excited. 'Why, I know that. I went there three times when I was a small boy – just for the day only, it's true, but I never forgot it. It's the dearest little cove you ever saw.'

'Let's go there then,' said Mike, at once.

But Mummy wanted to know more about it. 'Is the bathing safe? Does the tide come in too fast? Is the beach sandy or shingly?'

'The bathing's safe, the tide comes in quickly, but that doesn't matter, and the beach is golden sand – with shells all over it. Does that please you, Mummy?' said Daddy.

'And is there a good place for the caravans?' asked Mummy. 'Is there a farmhouse near for food? Is there . . .'

'Oh Mummy – just let's go, and we'll soon find out,' said Belinda. 'Sea-gull Cove – it sounds just right.'

'I'll pop down there and see if it's still as I remember it,' said Daddy. 'I'll go this week. In the meantime I'll arrange for another bunk to be put into the children's caravan for Benjy – he'll be coming tomorrow.'

The next day two men came along with some wood and went into the children's caravan. Mike, Belinda and Ann followed them in, staring. The caravan was quite crowded out then!

'We'll put the new bunk here – opposite the other bunks,' said the first man.

'Put it under the window, then Ben can look out,' said Belinda. 'Will it fold down to be out of the way in the daytime?'

'Oh yes,' said the man. 'Now – you'd better all get out of here, because when we start hammering and sawing we want a bit of space! My, these caravans are nice, aren't they? I wouldn't mind living in one myself. I suppose you wouldn't sell me this one, miss?'

'Oh *no*,' said Belinda. 'It's our home. We're the Caravan Family!'

'But we'll soon be the Seaside Family,' said Ann, going down the steps outside the caravan. 'Mike, Belinda – who's this? Is it Benjy?'

A small boy, a bit younger than Mike, was standing rather forlornly at the gate of the field, a large bag beside him. He was looking over at the caravans.

'Yes. It must be Benjy,' said Mike. None of the children had seen him before. He was just the son of a friend of Daddy's, and his mother was ill. That was all the children knew about him.

They went over to him. He didn't look very strong. He had straight fair hair and rather pale blue eyes, and a nice, sudden smile.

'Are you Benjy?' said Mike, and the boy nodded.

'Well, I'm Mike – and this is Belinda – and this is Ann – they're my sisters,' said Mike. 'Come along and I'll take you to our

mother. You're going to live with us for a bit, aren't you?'

'In our caravan. And we're just getting a bunk put in for you,' said Belinda.

'Don't you think you're lucky to be going to live in our caravan – a house on wheels?' said Ann.

'Well – I don't know,' said Benjy. 'I always thought it was gipsies who did that. I don't know that I'm going to like it. I'd rather live in a house.'

This was such a surprising remark to the three children that they stared at Benjy without a word. Ann felt cross. How could anyone possibly prefer a house to their colourful caravan?

Mike saw that Ann was going to say something that might sound rude to a visitor, so he spoke hurriedly.

'Come and see our mother. And I say – isn't it grand – we're all going off to the sea in two days' time!'

Ben's face brightened. 'Oh – that's better. We'll be in a hotel then, I suppose?'

'No. In our caravan,' said Ann. 'But if you don't like sleeping inside, you can sleep underneath!'

Benjy was just going to answer back when the children's mother came over to welcome him. She was so nice that Benjy was all smiles and politeness at once.

'You're just in time for a meal, Benjy,' she said. 'Such a nice one too – hard-boiled eggs and salad, and raspberries and cream! Will you like that?'

Benjy clearly thought that this was quite

all right. Belinda pulled Ann aside. 'Oh dear
– he'll *spoil* the holiday! How I do wish we
were going by ourselves. And I'll hate him in
our caravan! What a pity!'

CHAPTER THREE
Off to the Seaside

After their good meal of eggs and salad,
raspberries and cream, the children went to
show Benjy the caravan he was to share with
them. The men had now put in the new bunk,
and Mummy had put bedding on it. It looked
very nice.

'Come on Benjy – we'll show you
everything,' said Belinda. They all went into
the caravan. Belinda ran up the steps first. She
showed Benjy the door – it was cut in halves
in the middle, so that you could have just the
bottom half shut if you wanted to, and the
top half open, or both halves shut at once to
make a door.

The caravan looked so nice inside. It had highly polished cork carpet all over the floor, with red rugs on it. There was a little stove at one end for heating the caravan in winter. There was a small sink with taps, so that washing-up could be done.

'Isn't it marvellous, to have a sink and taps and water in a caravan?' said Ann, and she turned on a tap to show Benjy that real water came out. But he didn't think it was very wonderful.

'What's so grand about *that*?' he said. 'Water comes out of our taps at home too. I suppose you've got a water-tank on the roof, haven't you? Most caravans have.'

It was all very disappointing. Benjy hardly looked at the bunks. He patted his and made a face. 'A bit hard. Hope I shall sleep all right at night.'

'You ought to be thinking yourself jolly lucky to be sleeping in a bunk in a caravan,' said Ann, quite fiercely. Mike nudged her. This was Benjy's first day and he was still quite a new visitor. You didn't talk like that yet!

Nobody showed him the cupboards where things were kept so neatly. Nobody asked him to admire the row of cups and saucers and plates. Benjy didn't want to live in a caravan, so he wasn't going to admire anything about theirs at all. It was really very disappointing.

'You'll have to share our jobs,' said Mike, as they went down the caravan steps again. 'You know – help to get the wood in, and wash up ...'

'And make your own bunk and keep it tidy,' said Belinda.

'Goodness – can't you girls make the bunks by yourselves?' asked Benjy, rather scornfully. 'That's not a boy's work – making beds.'

'Our Daddy often makes up his own bunk, and if he can do it, so can you,' said Ann at once, and she put on a really terrible glare. Mummy was most astonished to see it when she met them round the corner of the caravan. Dear, dear – didn't her three want poor Benjy?

Two days went by very quickly. There was such a lot to do that the children didn't bother about Benjy and his ways very much. They had to go with their mother to buy beach clothes and swimming costumes, and they had to spend a day with Granny, who wanted to see them before they went. They had to go and fetch their two horses, Davey and Clopper, from the farmer, because they were to pull the caravans all the way to the sea.

Fortunately for Benjy he liked both Davey and Clopper! Ann really felt she might have smacked him if he had said something horrid about them.

'This is dear old Davey,' she said, patting the strong little black horse, that showed a white star on his forehead. 'He is awfully good and quiet – you can ride him.'

'And this is Clopper,' said Mike, leading up a dark brown and white horse. 'He's a very good horse – but he won't stand any nonsense. They're both darlings.'

'Oh, I like them,' said Benjy, and he stroked the velvety black nose that rested on his shoulder. 'Davey, I like you. And Clopper, you're a beauty. I love your shaggy feet. I say, Mike, let me drive your caravan, will you? I can make Clopper go as fast as anything.'

Daddy overheard him, 'Well, you won't drive old Clopper then,' he said, firmly. 'He's not a race horse! I shan't let you drive till I can trust you. Now, can you all be ready in an hour's time? I want to start for Sea-gull Cove then.'

Could they be ready? Of course they could!

Ann was ready in five minutes! She could always be quick when she really wanted to. Mike got the horses into harness. They stood patiently between their shafts, glad to be on the move once more.

Belinda went round picking up every scrap of litter. Mummy would never let one tiny bit of paper, or even a bit of egg-shell, be left in the field. Every corner had to be tidy and neat.

At last they were all ready. Daddy got up on the driving-seat of Davey's caravan. 'I'll go first, Mike, and show the way,' he called. 'Follow after me. Benjy, wait and shut the gate behind us.'

They were off – off to Sea-gull Cove by the sea! First went Daddy's caravan, with good old Davey pulling it – and then came

Clopper, driven by Mike, pulling the children's
caravan.

'We shall soon be the Seaside Family!' sang
Belinda. 'Hurrah, hurrah, for the Seaside
Family on its way to Sea-gull Cove!'

CHAPTER FOUR
Sea-gull Cove

It was exactly the right day to set off for the
seaside. The sun shone down hotly, and the
sky was bright blue except for little white
clouds here and there.

'I'm sure those clouds are made of cotton
wool,' said Ann, and that made everyone
laugh. They really did look like puffs of wool.

Davey and Clopper went steadily down the
country lanes. Daddy had looked up the best
way to go on his big maps, and he had chosen
the winding lanes rather than the main roads,
because then they wouldn't meet so much
traffic.

'And anyway the lanes are prettier than the

roads,' said Belinda. 'I love the way the red poppies nod at us as we go by, and the blue chicory flowers shine like little stars.'

'It takes longer to go by the lanes, Daddy says,' said Ann. 'But who minds that? If it takes longer than a day we can easily take our caravans into a field for the night and camp there!'

'Dear me, yes,' said Benjy. 'I hadn't thought we could do that. That might be rather fun!'

'You couldn't do that with a house,' said Mike, clicking to Clopper. 'A house has to stay put. It hasn't got wheels it can go wandering away on for miles and miles.'

'Still – I do prefer a house,' said Benjy, obstinately. 'I say, Mike, you might let me drive Clopper for a bit now.'

'No,' said Mike, firmly. 'Daddy said you can't

until he can trust you. I'm driving Clopper all day – unless I give the girls a turn.'

They went slowly down the little sunny lanes all day long. Daddy called a halt at teatime. 'We can't get to Sea-gull Cove today after all,' he said. 'We must camp in a meadow for the night. I can see a farmer over there. I'll ask him if we can stay here, in this field nearby.'

The farmer was nice. 'Yes, of course you can put up in my field,' he said. 'I can see you're the sort of folks I can trust not to set things on fire, or leave gates open. I'll send my boy out with eggs and milk, if you'd like them.'

They all spent a very happy evening in a field where big brown and white cows grazed, whisking their tails to keep away the flies.

'I wish I had a tail like a cow,' said Ann,

flapping at the flies over her head. 'I think it would be so very very useful!'

Davey and Clopper kept together away from the cows. They went to drink at the stream, and then they pulled at the juicy grass nearby. They looked happy and contented. They were tired after their long walk, pulling heavy caravans – and it was nice to eat and

drink and rest in a shady green field.

Ann came to give them each a lump of sugar. Benjy went with her. The horses nuzzled him and Ann, and blew down Benjy's neck. He was delighted.

'I wish they were mine,' he said to Ann. 'Fancy having two horses of your own like this. You *are* lucky!'

'You're nice when you talk like that,' said Ann. 'Instead of turning up your nose at everything!'

'Ann! Benjy! I want you to come and get into your bunks!' called Mummy. 'We're going to start off very early tomorrow morning, at half-past six. Come along quickly.'

Everyone was fast asleep before it was dark that night, even Mummy and Daddy! They were tired with their long drive and the sun and the breeze. Nobody heard the cows bumping into the children's caravan in the middle of the night, nobody even heard the screech owl that screamed and made Davey and Clopper almost jump out of their skins!

Daddy was awake at six o'clock. He looked out of the open door of the caravan. What a perfect morning! The sun was up, but still rather low, and the shadows of the trees were very long. Dew lay heavily on the grass.

Soon the whole family was having breakfast. Mummy had boiled the eggs from the farm, and there was creamy milk, new bread and farm butter with homemade strawberry jam. Everyone but Benjy ate two eggs each.

'What a poor appetite you've got, Benjy!' said Ann. 'No wonder you look so pale.'

'*I* think you're greedy!' said Benjy. 'Two eggs for breakfast! *I* can't think how you manage to eat them!'

'You wait for a few days – then you'll be like Mike, asking for *three* eggs, not two!' said Belinda.

They set off once more in the caravans.

Davey and Clopper plodded along steadily –
clippity-clop, clippity-clop.

Up hill and down hill, along pretty valleys,
round the honeysuckle hedges, past green
woods – and then, what a surprise!

They rounded a corner on a hill – and there
stretching below them was the sea – miles
upon miles of brilliant blue water!

'Oh – the SEA!' yelled Ann, and all the
children shouted for joy. The first sight was
always so exciting.

'And there's Sea-gull Cove!' cried Mike,
pointing. 'Look – it must be. Isn't it, Daddy?'

Yes, it was. There it lay, a little bay of
yellow sand and blue sea. On the beach sat
a crowd of sea-gulls. They rose into the air
and came gliding over the children's heads,
calling loudly.

'They're saying, "Welcome to Sea-gull Cove",' said Ann, pleased. 'They really are pleased to see us! Oh, what a lovely little place!'

CHAPTER FIVE
Settling in at Sea-gull Cove

The caravans went slowly down the hill to
Sea-gull Cove. It was a steep hill, and the
road wound round and about. Daddy and
Mike had to put on the brakes of the
caravans or they would have run down the
hill of their own accord and bumped the
horses along too fast!

The cove looked nicer and nicer as they
came nearer. 'The beach is simply *covered* with
shells!' called Mike.

'And look at the rockpools shining blue,'
said Belinda. 'How lovely to paddle in those.
They'll be as warm as anything.'

'We can have baths every single day from

morning to night,' said Ann.

'*I* shan't,' said Benjy at once. 'I'm not keen on bathing at all. Horrible cold water – and I can't swim, so I hate going in deep.'

'Can't *swim!*' said Ann, astonished. 'Why, I've been able to swim for ages and I'm much younger than you. You *are* a baby!'

Benjy went red and looked cross.

'Now he'll sulk,' said Belinda. 'Well, let him! He'll just *have* to learn to swim if he's going to enjoy himself here. My goodness, isn't the water blue!'

'Mike!' yelled back Daddy from his caravan in front. 'We'll take the caravans right down to the cove. There's a stretch of sandy grass at the back of the beach. If it's all right we'll have our caravans there.'

The children squealed for joy. 'Oh Daddy!'

shouted Belinda, 'how glorious! Perhaps the
tide will come almost up to our doors. We can
leave them open and lie and look at the sea
when we're in bed.'

The caravans were placed side by side on
the little grassy stretch behind the beach.
Davey and Clopper were led into a field
behind. Daddy set off to talk to the farmer
who owned the land nearby. He had already
seen him when he had gone down to Sea-
gull Cove for the day. He knew it was all
right to put the horses there. Now he
wanted to arrange for food and water for
his little family.

The children raced on to the sandy beach. It
was firm and golden beneath their bare feet.
Ann picked up some of the shells. 'Look – as
pink as a sunset! And do look at this one – it's

like a little trumpet. Oh, I shall make a most
beautiful collection of shells to take home
with me!'

Belinda and Mike ran down to the edge of
the sea. Little waves curled over each other just
there, and ran up the smooth, shining sand.
Farther out were bigger waves, curling over
with little splashes. The children yelled for joy.

'We'll bathe all day! We'll paddle! We'll get a boat and row! We'll shrimp and we'll fish! We'll ...'

Mike leapt into a bigger wave than usual and splashed Belinda from head to foot. Mummy called to him. 'Mike! If you're going to do that sort of thing come and get into swimming costumes! But first, don't you want something to eat?'

'Yes, if we can take it down to the very edge of the sea,' said Mike. He looked round for Benjy. Benjy was dabbling his toes in the edge of the water, looking rather solemn.

'Isn't it *lovely*, Benjy?' cried Belinda, rushing up to him, and giving him a little push that sent him running farther into the sea.

'Don't!' said Benjy, coming back in a hurry. 'My feet are awfully hot and the water's frightfully cold. I was just getting used to it.'

'I said, isn't it lovely!' cried Belinda, who was determined to make Benjy admire Sea-gull Cove.

'Well, it *looks* lovely – but won't it be rather lonely?' said Benjy. 'Shan't we be rather bored here all by ourselves?'

'Daddy says only stupid people are bored!' shouted Ann, in delight, coming up. 'So you must be stupid! Stupid baby!'

'Ann!' called Mummy, really shocked. 'Don't be so rude to Benjy. Let him get used to things.'

'Well, he must get used to us too, then,' said Ann. 'Mummy, how *can* he ask if we'll be bored in this lovely, lovely place?'

'Ann,' said Mummy, pulling her quietly to one side. 'Do remember that Benjy is very fond of his mother, and I expect that, although he doesn't say much about it, he is secretly very worried about her – she is terribly ill, you know.'

'Oh dear,' said Ann. 'I quite forgot. I'm sorry, Mummy. I'll try and remember to be nice to him. All the same, he's a silly baby.'

Soon all four children were in their swimming costumes. Mummy gave them a basket of food to take down to the very edge of the sea.

'Let's go and sit in the water and have our dinner,' said Belinda, with a giggle. 'I've never in my life had a picnic sitting in the water.'

So they went and sat down in the edge of the sea – all except Benjy, who thought it was a horrid idea. They ate their ham sandwiches and nibbled their tomatoes

happily, while tiny waves ran up their legs
and all round their bodies.

'Lovely!' said Mike, popping the last of his
tomato into his mouth. 'Hurrah for Sea-gull
Cove – the nicest place in the world!'

CHAPTER SIX
Benjy has a Lesson

The tide came in all that afternoon. It crept up the beach bit by bit, and the children watched eagerly to see if it would reach the caravans. But it didn't of course.

'Do you think it might if we had a storm, Daddy?' asked Ann, longingly. 'Oh, Daddy – do you suppose the water would ever get to the top of the wheels, so that the two caravans would float away like Noah's Arks?'

'Oooh – that *would* be fun!' said Belinda.

'That would never happen,' said Daddy, firmly. 'Because if there were a storm I should at once move the caravans farther back!'

'Oh Daddy – you're a spoil-sport!' said Ann, with a laugh. 'Just think of us all floating gaily away on the sea!'

'How horrid!' said Benjy, with a shiver.

'Benjy's afraid of adventures,' said Ann. 'He doesn't even like going into the water up to his knees. He ...'

'Ann!' said Mummy, sharply. 'Have you already forgotten what I said?'

Ann went red. 'Oh dear – I'm so sorry,' she said.

'Well, please don't forget again,' said Mummy. 'I don't like being cross on a holiday. Now, what are you going to do? Paddle, dig, bathe, or what?'

'Bathe,' said Mike, at once. 'I want a good long swim. Coming, Daddy?'

'Rather!' said Daddy, 'and Mummy will too.

I'll give Benjy his first lesson in swimming too,
I think.'

Benjy looked up in alarm. 'I don't think I
want to learn to swim,' he said.

'Rubbish!' said Daddy. 'All children must
learn to swim. Look at Ann here – she swims
like a little fish.'

'I can even swim under water,' said Ann,
proudly. 'It's easy! I can open my eyes under
water too, and see the things on the bottom of
the sand.'

'Can you really?' said Benjy, amazed. 'I
should like to do that!' He turned to Ann's
father. 'All right, sir, I'll do my best to learn.
But don't duck me or anything, will you?'

'You can trust Daddy,' said Belinda, at once.
'He'll always tell you what he's going to do.'

So Benjy had his first lesson. He was afraid

when he had to walk right into the water up
to his waist. He said it was cold, he said it was
too deep, he said he was sure there were crabs
waiting to bite his toes!

'Yes, it does seem a bit cold,' agreed Daddy.
'And it is quite deep for you. And there may
be one or two crabs. But we just won't bother
about any of those things at all. Now then
– bend forward – that's right – up with your
legs! Don't struggle. I've got you safely. Can't

you feel my hand under your tummy?'

Benjy really was very frightened, but he tried his best to do what Daddy said. He worked his arms and legs furiously, and got completely out of breath. The other children roared with laughter at him.

'Daddy, he's trying to go at sixty miles an hour!' squealed Ann. 'You'll have to give him a hooter or something if he goes at that pace!'

That made Benjy laugh too, and he swallowed a mouthful of water and choked. He struck out with his arms in alarm, and clung to Daddy quickly.

'There – you're all right and you did quite well,' said Daddy. 'Now walk into the shallower water while we all go out for a swim.'

Then the Caravan Family all went for a

swim together. They went into deep water, and not even Daddy could feel the sand below with his feet. Ann felt very brave indeed. Then she gave a sudden scream and Daddy looked round at once.

'Oh! Oh! Something's nibbling me! OH!'

Daddy swum up to her and then he turned over on his back and roared with laughter as he floated there.

'Look what's nibbling Ann!' he shouted to the others, and he held up a strand of ribbon seaweed! 'It was bobbing against her – and she thought it was nibbling her! Oh, Ann – how does seaweed nibble?'

It was such fun in the water. But soon Daddy led the way back to the shore, striking out strongly. 'It's the first time we've been swimming for a long time,' he called. 'We

won't overdo it – we shall be so stiff tomorrow
if we do. Come along to the beach and we'll
have some races to warm us up.'

They went to the sandy beach. Benjy was
there waiting for them, shivering. Daddy
made them all race up and down, up and

down, and soon they were warm and glowing.

'The tide's almost up to the caravan steps, it is really, look!' cried Ann, in delight. Everyone looked. It was about twelve feet away from the steps, but the water was already going down. It certainly wouldn't reach the caravans *that* evening!

Belinda gave a terrific yawn. Mummy heard her. 'You're all tired out with excitement,' she said. 'We'll have a light supper – and then off to bed!'

Funnily enough nobody minded going to bed early. 'You see,' said Ann, 'it's going to be *such* a treat lying in our bunks, Mummy, and looking out at the evening sea – and watching it get darker and darker!'

But she didn't see it getting darker – she was sound asleep!

CHAPTER SEVEN
Everything is Lovely

Next morning Mike awoke first. He couldn't think what the noise was just outside. Lap-lap-lap, plish-plash-plash!

And then he remembered – of course, they were by the sea. THE SEA! He sat up in his bunk and looked out. The tide was in again, and was lapping some yards away from the caravan steps. Plish-plish-plash! The sun shone over the great stretch of water and made bright sparkles on it everywhere.

Mike took a deep breath. It was all so clean and new. Surely the world never never looked so lovely as it did in the very early morning.

There came a rush of big wings, and Mike

saw a sea-gull standing in the edge of the water. It was facing the caravan. He held his breath because it began to walk towards the steps!

It was a magnificent bird, snow-white and pearl-grey with bright, alert eyes. It walked up to the caravan and then hopped up a step – then another step – then another! And at last it was on the top step of all, peering into the caravan, its head on one side!

'Eeee-ooo, eee-ooo, eee-ooo!' it screamed suddenly, as if it were asking for breakfast. Mike almost jumped out of his skin. The other three awoke in a fright and sat up. They stared in surprise at the enormous sea-gull. It flapped its great wings and soared away into the air. 'Eee-ooo, eee-ooo, eee-ooo!' it squealed, almost as if it were laughing at them.

'Goodness – that did scare me!' said Ann, with a laugh. 'Did it come to say good morning or what, Mike?'

'It's awfully tame,' said Mike. 'We'll feed the gulls today with bread, and see if we can get them to take it from our hands. I really thought that gull was going to walk into the caravan! I say – what about a bathe before breakfast?'

'Horrid!' said Benjy. But the others didn't think so and they scrambled into bathing things and tore down to the water at once. It was cold – but who minded that? Well, Benjy did, of course, but as he didn't put more than his toes into the water, he didn't even shiver.

Mummy called to him. 'Benjy – if you're not going to bathe, come and help me with breakfast. And you might see if you can find

some driftwood on the beach, thrown up
by the tide. We'll have to find some wood
somewhere for the fire, and stack it in the sun
to dry.'

Benjy had already found that there were
plenty of odd jobs to do if you lived in a
caravan. He had learnt to make his own
bed – or rather his bunk – each day. He had
been ticked off for leaving the tap running
so that the water-tank had emptied. He had
had to sweep the floor several times and
shake the mats.

He was beginning not to mind doing
all these little jobs. Everyone else did them
cheerfully, and after all they weren't very
much bother. All the same he made up his
mind that Mike would have to do his share of
hunting for driftwood and bringing it to stack

in the sun for the fire!

'I want to buy a boat to sail on the rockpools,' said Belinda at breakfast. They were having it on the beach. Daddy had lighted a wood-fire to boil the kettle and cook the eggs. 'Can I go to the nearest village and see if I can get one, Mummy?'

'And I want a shrimping-net,' said Mike. 'I bet I could catch enough shrimps to cook for tea each day!'

'Oooh, lovely,' said Belinda. 'I do like shrimps with brown bread and butter. Do *you* want to buy anything at the shops, Benjy?'

'I'll see,' said Benjy. 'I might buy a big ball if I can see one. This is a good beach for a ball.'

'And I shall buy ice-creams for everyone,' said Ann.

'We won't be *too* long at the village,' said

Belinda. 'We simply mustn't waste a single hour away from Sea-gull Cove if we can help it. Mummy, can I throw some bread to the gulls now? You've got half a stale loaf there.'

The gulls were standing not far off, watching the children eating. Mummy broke the stale loaf into bits and gave it to the four children. One by one they threw bits to the gulls.

They came nearer and nearer, squealing angrily if one gull got too many pieces. They pecked one another if they thought one had been unfair. 'Just like naughty children,' said Mummy.

'You know, if we get the gulls much tamer than this, we'll have to lock up all our food,' said Daddy. 'They will be into the caravans before we know where we are! Hey you big fellow, that's my toe, not a bit of bread!'

'Well,' said Mummy, getting up and scaring off the gulls at once, 'it's time we cleared away. Mike, there is a bus you can catch up the hill there in half an hour's time. Girls, wash up for me. Boys, make the bunks and look for wood. I'm going to the farm for food.'

Soon the little family was busy about its tasks, chattering happily. 'Now for the bus!' said Mike at last. 'Come on, or we'll miss it! Run, Benjy, or you'll be left behind!'

CHAPTER EIGHT
Benjy's Ball

They just caught the bus nicely, and off
they went, jolting through the country lanes
to the nearest village of Minningly. It was
a dear little place, with only four shops,
a church, a chapel, and clusters of pretty
thatched houses.

'It must be fun to live in a tiny place like
this and know simply *everybody*,' said Ann. 'I
should like that.'

'Look – there's a shop where we can buy
what we want,' said Mike. 'It looks as if it sells
simply *everything*!'

So it did. It was a little general shop, hung
with all kinds of things inside and out – pails,

kettles, rope, sou'westers, china, wire-netting, postcards, sweets, ships, toys – everything was there it seemed!

'Is there anything you *don't* sell?' Ann asked the little round woman who beamed at them from behind a counter piled high with yet more goods.

'Oh yes, miss,' she said. 'I don't sell rocking horses and I don't sell cuckoo clocks – so don't you go asking for them now, will you?'

Ann giggled. 'I wasn't going to,' she said. 'I really want to buy some ice-cream.'

'Ah, I've plenty of *that*!' said the plump little woman, and she took the lid from a big ice-cream container. She scooped yellow ice-cream into four cornets. It looked lovely. Ann paid her in delight.

'*Just* what we wanted!' she said. 'Can we

look round your exciting shop while we
eat them?'

'Of course – and you can poke into any of
the corners you like,' said the shop-woman.
'There's no knowing what you might find!'

Belinda found just the ship she wanted –
one with a nice heavy keel that looked as
if it would help the ship to sail properly and
not fall on its side. Mike found a splendid
shrimping-net – a good strong one that
wouldn't break if he pressed it too hard into
the sand when he went shrimping.

And you should have seen the ball that
Benjy bought! It really was the nicest the four
had ever seen! It was blown up to make it
very big and bouncy. It was striped in yellow
and red and blue and was twice as big as a
football!

'That's a lovely ball to play with in the sea,' said the little shop-woman, when Benjy paid her. 'It bobs on the water like a live thing.'

'Oh, I shan't play with it on the sea,' said Benjy, at once. 'It's too precious. I shall only play with it on the sands.'

'I say – we'd better hurry if we want to catch the bus back,' said Mike, suddenly. 'Look – it's at the corner there, waiting. Goodbye – we did enjoy your shop!'

Off they went, scurrying to the bus, and it was not long before they were back at dear old Sea-gull Cove again. Daddy was waiting for them.

'Coming in for a bathe?' he shouted. 'And what about your swimming lesson, Benjy? You'll get on fine today!'

'I don't think I want one today,' said Benjy.

'I think I'd rather play with my new ball – isn't it a beauty?'

'Rather!' said Daddy. 'You can play with it after your lesson – we all will, to get ourselves warm. Come along now, into your swimming trunks!'

And so Benjy had his second lesson, and he splashed away valiantly. Daddy was quite pleased with him. 'Now listen to me, Benjy,' he said. 'You want to practise the strokes I have told you. Practise them by yourself in the water each day – three or four times a day.'

'Benjy won't! He never goes in farther than his knees!' shouted Ann. 'He's afraid!'

'Well – if he does not go in farther than that it'll take him a long time to learn to swim!' said Daddy. 'Now come on out, all of you – and we'll have a fine game with Benjy's new ball!'

It certainly was a lovely ball. It bounced as lightly as a feather, and was so light that even the wind could bowl it over the sand. The children had to run fast after it when the breeze began to join in their game!

They were all terribly hungry for dinner. Mummy had bought a big meat pie from the farm, and it was soon gone. Not even a small piece was left for the gulls! Then plums and greengages were handed out, and if anyone wanted bread-and-butter with them they could have it. Creamy milk from the farm was in a big jug set in a pail of cold water to keep it cool.

'Lovely!' said Ann, when she had finished. 'Now for another bathe.'

'Not after that enormous lunch,' said
Mummy firmly. 'You can bathe at three
o'clock, but not before. Have a read now,
in the shade. That would be nice. Lend
Benjy a book.'

At three o'clock Mike, Ann, Daddy, Mummy
and Belinda were all out in the water again
– they really were a family of fishes! Benjy
wouldn't come. He played on the beach with
his ball.

And then something happened. The wind
took the big ball and blew it down to the
edge of the sea. It bobbed on the water. It was
taken out a little way. Benjy splashed in after
it – but the wind took it out even farther!
'Mike! Belinda! Get my ball!' squealed Benjy.
But nobody heard him, nobody at all.

Now what was he to do? He would lose
his ball – there it went, bobbing away on the
waves! Poor Benjy!

CHAPTER NINE
Benjy is Most Surprising

Benjy stood in the water up to his knees and howled dismally. 'My ball! Get my ball! It's going away on the water. MIKE! MIKE!'

But Mike didn't hear him. Mike was trying to swim under water with Ann. Daddy and Mummy were having a race on their own. Belinda was floating peacefully on her back. Nobody saw what was happening to Benjy.

Benjy stared desperately at his bobbing ball. It came back a little way because a wave broke over it and sent it rolling in towards the beach. If only it would come back a little more Benjy might be able to reach it.

He waded in deeper. Oooh – he was up to

his waist now. How dangerous, he thought –
and how cold! Ah, there was his ball – nearer
still! Another few steps and he really might get
it. He waded deeper still. Now he was almost
up to it – and oh joy, a wave sent the ball
almost on top of him. He had it! It was safe!

He felt very proud indeed. He had never
been out so deep before. A wave wetted him
right to the armpits. After all, the water wasn't
so very cold – it was rather warm and felt

silky to the skin. He waded back with his ball
and put it in a safe place. Then he turned and
looked at the sea.

The others were really having a glorious
time out there. It was fun to hear them
shouting and laughing. What a pity he
couldn't swim!

Benjy waded into the sea again. It still felt
warm. He waded right up to his waist. Then
he bobbed under to wet his shoulders. Why, it

was *lovely*! He stayed under for a little while and then began to make the armstrokes he had been shown that morning.

He suddenly lost his balance and his legs went up into the water. He struck out in alarm – and goodness gracious, he really could hardly believe it, but he swam three whole strokes before water went into his mouth and he choked!

Benjy was full of pride and amazement. He had swum – he really had! His feet had been right up in the water. Should he try again?

And then he saw the others nearby watching him in astonishment.

'Benjy! We saw you then! Were you really swimming?' yelled Ann.

'Benjy, do it again!' shouted Mike, swimming up. 'I say – you didn't *really* swim, did you?'

'I did,' said Benjy. 'I'll show you!'

He let his legs leave the sandy bottom and then he struck out again. Four strokes this time before he went under, spluttering and gasping.

'Daddy, he's marvellous!' cried Belinda. 'Mummy, look, he's learnt already! If he practises he'll soon be swimming out with us! How lovely!'

Benjy had never felt so proud in his life. He had always been a spoilt timid boy – now for the first time he had been really brave on his own, and he felt grand. He did some more strokes, and then went under so completely that he really thought he was drowning!

'We're going in now,' said Mike helping him up to the surface. 'I say – don't swallow *all* the sea, will you? We do want a bit left, you know.'

'Can we play with your lovely ball, Benjy?' asked Ann, wading out with the spluttering Benjy.

'Yes, of course,' said Benjy.

'Benjy, whatever made you go and swim like that all by yourself?' asked Belinda curiously. 'I never thought you would. You *are* brave!'

Benjy nearly didn't say anything about his

runaway ball. He badly wanted to be thought brave enough to go and practise all on his own, without any ball to make him wade into the water.

But he knew that Mike and the others always owned up and never pretended, and he wanted to be the same. So he went red and told them what had happened.

'I wasn't really brave! It was my new ball that made me go into the water. The wind blew it out to sea, and you didn't hear me calling to you to get it for me. So I waded out and got it – and it was so nice out there I thought I'd practise swimming. That's all. I wasn't really *brave*, you see.'

Daddy had heard all this. He clapped Benjy on the shoulder. 'It's nice to see a boy brave enough to own up that it was his ball sent him into the water, and nothing else – and very nice to see that he was sensible enough to stay there once he was in! I'm pleased with you Benjy. You'll be as fine a swimmer as Mike soon!'

Well, of course that was quite enough to make Benjy determined to practise his swimming every single day. He blushed with pride and thought the children's father was the nicest he'd ever met – except his own, of course.

They all had great fun that day. They sailed Belinda's boat on the pool, and it really did sail beautifully and only fell over once on its side, when the wind blew too strongly.

Mike went shrimping and caught seventy-two shrimps and Mummy cooked them for supper. The gulls came round and ate up all the heads and tails that nobody wanted!

'They're quite useful, aren't they?' said Ann, throwing them a few more heads from her plate. 'Good as dustmen, the way they clear up our litter! No, shoo, gull – you are *not* to peck Belinda's boat!'

'What fun we're having!' said Mike. 'I wish these holidays would never, never end!'

CHAPTER TEN

Ann and Benjy

Now the days began to slip by too quickly.
'I never know *what* day of the week it is now,'
said Mike. 'I really thought today was Tuesday
– and now I find it's Friday! Goodness knows
where Wednesday and Thursday went to!'

'We know when it's Sunday, anyway,' said
Ann, 'because then we hear the church bell
ringing from the village of Minningly – and
we go to church.'

'Yes – I liked that,' said Belinda. 'It's the
dearest little church I ever went into – the sort
of church that God really does feel near in.'

'We never go to church at home,' said Benjy,
'but I liked going with you. God never feels

very near to me though. I'm sure He doesn't bother about a boy like me. I say "Our Father" at night, but I never ask Him for things like you do. I can't really feel that He's listening.'

'Well, you can't feel very safe then,' said Ann. 'I mean – we always feel that God really *is* a Father and loves us, and is always looking after us, so we feel safe. But you can't feel at all safe.'

'Well, I don't,' said Benjy. 'I'm always afraid something awful is going to happen, and – well, don't let's talk about it.'

'But I want to,' said Ann. 'Mike and Belinda, you go away. I do really want to talk to Benjy. I don't like his not feeling safe.'

Mike and Belinda went off. They were rather bored with this anyway. They just thought Benjy was being silly, as usual.

But he wasn't. Something was frightening him very much. He told Ann what it was.

'It's my mother,' he said. 'You know she's awfully ill, Ann. I haven't always been very kind to her, and now what's worrying me all the time is that she might – she might *die*, Ann, and I wouldn't even have been able to tell her I was sorry.'

'Oh Benjy!' said Ann. 'Might she really die? And you're away here with us and can't even tell her you love her and didn't ever mean to be horrid? Oh Benjy, I'm sorry I've been horrid to *you*. I ought to have been kind. I shall pray for ever so long tonight to ask God to make your mother better. You must too. God will know it's very important if we both pray for exactly the same thing for a long time.'

'Well, I will,' said Benjy. 'Don't tell your father and mother about this, Ann. You see, I heard them talking yesterday when they didn't know I was near — and they said my mother was worse. I couldn't help hearing.'

'Ann! Benjy! Whatever are you talking about so earnestly?' called Mummy. 'Not planning any mischief, I hope!'

'No, Mummy,' said Ann. She gave Benjy a quick hug. 'Don't worry any more. You needn't now.'

'ANN! Come on — Daddy's got a boat and we're going out on it!' shouted Mike. 'Do come.'

Ann was thrilled. She raced down to the sea, where Daddy had the boat. Benjy went too, looking much more cheerful. He hadn't liked Ann a bit before – but now he felt as if she was his best friend. He got into the boat with the others.

'Can you row?' Mike asked him. Benjy shook his head.

'But I'd like to learn,' he said, rather surprisingly.

'Good boy!' said Mike, and grinned at him. 'You're not nearly such a mutt as you were, are you?'

Rowing was hard work, Benjy found. All the others rowed well, even Ann. It really was astonishing, the things these three could do! They were always willing to try anything and go on trying till they were good at it.

They had a bathe from the boat itself.
'Ooooh! *Really* deep water here!' said Mike,
and dived over the edge of the boat. Splash!
He was up again at once. Belinda dived in
too, but Ann let herself down over the side.
Benjy looked at Ann's father.

'Shall I go in too, sir?'

'Yes, if you like,' said the children's father.
'If you get into trouble I'll dive in and get
you. You can swim now – it doesn't matter
whether you're in deep or shallow water, you
can still swim!'

So in went Benjy, and although it gave
him an odd feeling at first to know that the
bottom of the sea was rather far down, he
soon forgot it. He forgot his troubles too, and
Ann was very pleased to hear him squealing
with laughter.

Then back they went to the shore again, and the day slipped by as quickly as usual. It seemed no time at all before it was bedtime.

Benjy and Ann were sent to bed first because they were the youngest. 'Hurry, Benjy,' said Ann. 'Then we can have a long time to say our prayers before the others come. You know how important it is tonight.'

And so, if Ann's mother had looked in ten minutes later she would have seen two washed and brushed children kneeling down beside one of the bunks, absolutely still. How hard they were praying!

'Please, dear God, think how sad Benjy is and make his mother better,' prayed Ann. 'You always want to be kind, so I know You'll help poor Benjy. Please, please make his mother better!'

It was the longest prayer Benjy and Ann
had ever made. 'Goodnight, Benjy,' said Ann,
when she climbed into her bunk. 'God was
listening, as he always does. Here come the
other two – we only *just* finished in time!'

CHAPTER ELEVEN
About Sea-creatures – and a Telegram!

Next day Benjy waited eagerly for the postman. Would there be good news? He had no letter, but there was one for the children's mother.

'Yes, Benjy,' she said, when she saw him looking anxiously at her. 'It's about your mother. She's just the same, neither better nor worse.'

'There you are,' Benjy said miserably to Ann, when they were alone. 'I told you so. God doesn't really care about a boy like me.'

'It's wicked to say things like that,' said Ann. 'Don't let's talk about it if that's what you think. Look, what's that – it's a starfish! Daddy, come and look!'

Everyone came and looked at the unusual five-fingered creature. 'It's just five legs and a tummy!' said Daddy. 'Its mouth is in the middle of it.'

'How does it get along?' asked Mike, seeing the creature dragging itself down the sand.

Daddy turned it over. The children saw dozens of white tube-like things sticking out of the five fingers. 'Those are its legs,' said Daddy. 'Look at the way it puts them out. It takes hold of the ground with the first rows, pulls itself up, takes hold with the back legs, and so it gets along. Very clever!'

The starfish got into a pool and disappeared. A crab ran out as if it was afraid. It sank itself into the soft wet sand and vanished.

'That's another clever little creature!'
said Mike, with a laugh. 'I wish I could
make myself disappear like that. Daddy,
how do crabs grow? Their hard shell can't
grow, surely?'

'Oh no,' said Daddy. 'The poor crab has
to creep into a dark corner and hide himself
when he grows too big for his shell. Then his
shell splits – and out he wriggles! He hides
away quietly for a day or two – and hey
presto, a completely new shell grows on
his body!'

'It's just like magic,' said Ann. 'I wish I could
see it happening. Daddy, I'm going shrimping
if Mike will let me borrow his net. Then you
can tell me about shrimps and prawns too!'

She went off with Mike's net, and soon
she and Benjy were hard at work catching

shrimps and prawns in the big rockpools.

They looked at their peculiar eyes on stalks, and their funny little bunches of swimmeret legs. 'Daddy told me that the shrimps and prawns are the dustmen of these rockpools.' said Ann. 'They clear up all the rubbish. Did you know that, Benjy? Oh, do look – there are some sea-anemones!'

They both looked at the different jelly-like lumps growing in red and green on the rock in the water. 'Watch!' said Ann. 'They will put out things that look like petals soon, and wave them about in the water. Mummy, look! What are those sea-anemones doing?'

'Ah, they are trying to trap tiny shrimps or other creatures in those waving petals,' said Mummy. 'Once they have caught them with those unusual arms of theirs they will drag them into their middles – and that's the end of the little shrimps! They're not flowers, of course, they are jelly-like creatures that are always hungry!'

'Can I give this one a bit of bread?' asked Ann. 'Here you are, anemone. Take that! Mummy, he's got it – his petals caught hold of it – and he's dragged it into his middle part. Goodness, I'm glad I'm not a shrimp in this pool!'

'Yes, it would be dangerous,' agreed Benjy, and he gently touched the petals of the sea-anemone. 'I can feel this one catching hold of my finger! No, anemone – you're not going to gobble it up!'

The day went quickly by and soon it was teatime. Belinda set the tablecloth out on the beach, and she and Ann put out the tea – two loaves of new bread, a big slab of farm butter, a chocolate cake from the farm, made that morning, and an enormous jar of homemade jam. What a tea!

They all sat down to enjoy it. In the middle of it Benjy looked, and gave an exclamation.

'The telegraph boy! Oh dear – do you think he wants *us*?'

Everyone's heart sank. Daddy and Mummy looked at one another. They were afraid of what the telegram might say.

Poor Benjy went very pale. Ann squeezed his arm. 'It's all right,' she said. 'You'll see, it will be all right.'

The boy came up on his bicycle. Daddy took the telegram. Everyone watched him tear it open, his face grave. Then he suddenly smiled.

'Benjy! Your mother's better! She'll get well!'

'Oh!' squealed all the children, and Benjy sat smiling with tears running down his cheeks.

'You do look funny, Benjy, smiling and crying too,' said Ann. 'Oh, Benjy, I was right, wasn't I? Benjy, I'm so glad for you. Mummy, do look at him – I've never seen anyone

laughing and crying at once before.'

'Don't be horrid, Ann,' said Mike.

'She's not,' said Benjy, in a shaky voice. 'You don't know how good and kind she is. It's all because of Ann that I'm happy again. Now I shall *really* enjoy my holiday!'

CHAPTER TWELVE
Goodbye to Sea-gull Cove!

Benjy was so full of high spirits after the
good news that he made everyone laugh. He
shouted, he paddled up to his waist, he turned
head-over-heels in the water, he even swam
fifty strokes out to sea and back, a thing he
had never done before.

'Poor Benjy,' said Mummy, watching him.
'He must have been very miserable about his
mother – and we didn't guess it.'

'Ann knew,' said Mike. 'Good old Ann.
Hallo, here comes Benjy again, with his
ball. All right Benjy, I'll play with you.
Race you to the cliff and back, kicking the
ball all the way!'

Benjy didn't say much to Ann about his feelings, because he was shy. 'I just want to say that I feel as if God's given me another chance now,' he said. 'I shall be awfully good to my mother to make up for my horridness before. Ann – wasn't it marvellous that our prayers were answered like that?'

'Yes, but I really did believe they would be,' said Ann. 'And that's important too, Benjy, don't forget. Benjy, do you like living in a caravan now? You didn't at first.'

'I love it,' said Benjy, promptly.

'Do you like sleeping in a bunk?' asked Ann.

'I love it,' said Benjy.

'Do you mind making the bunks and getting in the wood and things like that?' went on Ann.

'I love it,' said Benjy. 'Go on, I shall say "I

love it" to everything you ask me, silly – don't you know I'm happy here?'

'Do you like polishing the floor of our caravan?' asked Ann, slyly. This was always her job.

'I love it,' said Benjy, of course.

'All right – you go and do it then for a change!' squealed Ann. And oddly enough, Benjy took the polishing duster and went off like a lamb. Well, well – he really was a different boy, there was no doubt about that!

And now the holidays really did seem to fly past. There were two days of rain, when the children sat and played games in the caravan and really enjoyed the change. They bathed in the rain too, and that was fun. There was one day that was so hot that nobody dared to sit out in the sun, and Ann expected to see the sea begin to boil! But fortunately it didn't!

Benjy astonished everyone by his sudden appetite. He demanded two eggs at breakfast-time – and one day he asked for three!

'Aha!' said Mummy, 'what did I tell you? Yes, you can have another – but don't ask for *four* tomorrow, or there won't be enough.'

Then the last week came. Then the day before the last, when the children did simply everything they could so as not to miss anything.

'We'll dig and paddle and bathe and sail the little boat, and shrimp and go rowing and collect shells and seaweed,' said Belinda. 'Oh, I do hate it when holidays come to an end – it's just as horrid as the beginning is nice!'

And then the last day came. Oh dear! Come along Davey and Clopper, your holiday is over too. What – you are glad? You want to get back to the old field you know so well – you will enjoy the long pull home?

Seaweed hung in long strips from the outside walls of the caravans. The children were taking the fronds home to tell the weather.

'If the seaweed's dry the weather will be fine; if it gets damp, it shows rain is coming,' said Ann to Benjy. 'You can take the very

nicest bits home with you to show your mother, Benjy.'

'I've had a lovely time,' said Benjy. 'I thought at first I was going to hate it, and I didn't much like any of you – but I've loved it, and I feel as if you were my very best friends.'

Then Mike made them jump. 'Football!' he said suddenly. 'I've just remembered – it'll be the Christmas term now, with football. And there'll be gym. I like that.'

'And we shall have hockey,' said Belinda. 'And we're going to do a play – aren't we Ann? We're both going to be in one at school.'

Everyone suddenly cheered up. Holidays were lovely – but there were things at school that you didn't have at any other time. There were so many others there too – there was always something going on. It would be fun to go back.

Davey and Clopper were put into the shafts. Daddy called to Benjy. 'You and Mike can take it in turns to drive Clopper, Benjy. I can trust you all right now.'

'I can trust you all right now.' What lovely words to hear. It was the nicest thing in the world to be trusted. Benjy would see that his mother could trust him now, too. He looked round at the golden beach. He was sad to leave it – but all good things come to an end.

'Come on, Benjy!' called Mike. 'We're going.'

Up the hill went the two caravans, pulled by good old Davey and Clopper. The sea-

gulls came swooping round them. 'Eee-ooo, eee-ooo, eee-oooo!' they called.

'They're shouting goodbye,' said Ann, in delight. 'Goodbye! We'll come again. Don't forget us, will you, because we'll come again. Goodbye!'

The Caravan Family

Join Mike, Belinda and Ann in a fun-filled summer adventure from Enid Blyton!

Out Now!

When Dad buys two caravans for everyone to live in, the family set off on some amazing adventures.

Available now in all good bookshops and online

www.egmont.co.uk

EGMONT

Discover the magical worlds of
Enid Blyton

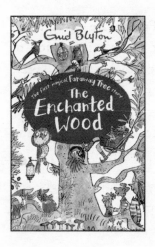

Joe, Beth and Frannie move to the country and find an Enchanted Wood right on their doorstep! And in the wood stands the magic Faraway Tree where the Saucepan Man, Moon-Face and Silky the fairy live.

Together they visit the strange lands which lie at the top of the tree and where they have the most exciting adventures!

Rick thought it would be dull in the country with Joe, Beth and Frannie. But that was before he found the magic Faraway Tree!

They only have to climb through the cloud at the top of the huge, magical tree to be in the Land of Spells, or the Land of Topsy-Turvy, or even the Land of Do-As-You-Please!

Discover the magical worlds of
Enid Blyton

Joe, Beth and Frannie are fed up when they hear that Connie is coming to stay – she's so stuck-up and bossy. But that won't stop them from having exciting adventures with their friends Silky the fairy, Moon-Face and Saucepan Man.

Together they climb through the cloud at the top of the tree and visit all sorts of strange places!

One day, Robin and Joy read about the Magic Faraway Tree in a book and decide to go meet Joe, Beth and Frannie themselves. The five children have all sorts of exciting adventures together, including being captured by the Enchanter Red-Cloak in the Land of Castles, a birthday treat for Joy in the Land of Wishes, and a delicious visit to the Land of Cakes!